CLUB MOTTOS

Welcome to the clubs, B.B.s! Ready to test your code-breaking skills? Every club in this book has a motto written in top secret code. When you figure the mottos out, you can write them below. Find them all and you're officially ready to run the world!

24K GOLD	POP
ART	RETRO
ATHLETIC	ROCK
CHILL OUT	SLEEPOVER
COSPLAY	SPIRIT
DANCE	SPOOKY
ELEKTRO	S.T.E.M.
GLAM	STORYBOOK
GLEE	SWIM
GLITTERATI	THEATER
HIP-HOP	
NAP	
OPPOSITES	

You can take this page out of the book so you don't have to keep flipping back to it.
Answers can be found in the back of the book.

What's a motto?

Don't know. What's a motto with you?

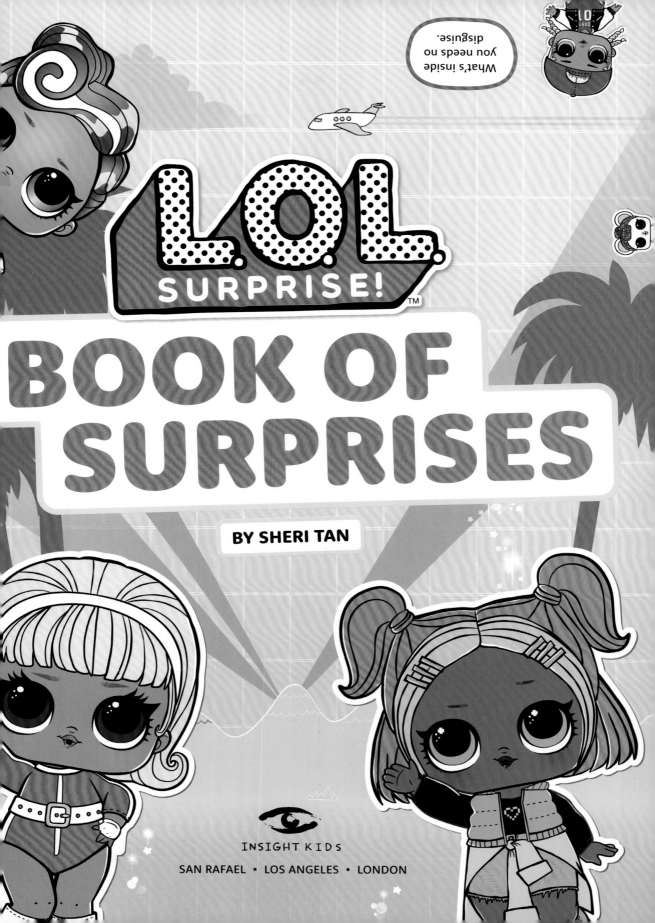

L.O.L. SURPRISE! ™

BOOK OF SURPRISES

BY SHERI TAN

What's inside you needs no disguise.

INSIGHT KIDS

SAN RAFAEL • LOS ANGELES • LONDON

Welcome to L.O.L. Surprise!, where B.B.s run the world! We're glitter and glam, sparkly and smart, and always ready to take on whatever life throws our way. We love what we do, and there's no stopping us—ever!

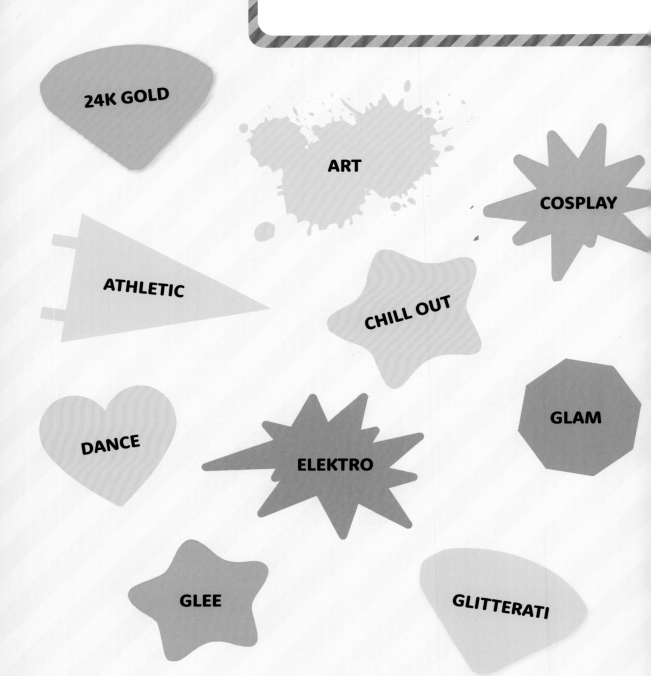

24K GOLD

ART

COSPLAY

ATHLETIC

CHILL OUT

DANCE

ELEKTRO

GLAM

GLEE

GLITTERATI

HIP HOP

NAP

OPPOSITES

POP

RETRO

ROCK

SLEEPOVER

SPIRIT

SWIM

STORYBOOK

SPOOKY

S.T.E.M.

THEATER

TINY TOYS

No matter color, shape, or size.

24K GOLD CLUB
BOLD AND GOLD!

All that glitters . . . is definitely gold! Why settle for anything less? Always ready to shine, these sparkly B.B.s have hearts as pure as the club's name and love to show the world just how priceless they are!

CLUB MOTTO

PAMPERED PET
Lucky Luxe's favorite bedtime story is *Goldilocks and the Three Bears*.

| LUXE | LUCKY LUXE | #INSTABUNNY | #INSTAGOLD |

SURPRISE!
The first gold rush in the United States started in 1799 in North Carolina when a twelve-year-old boy found a gold nugget that weighed 17 pounds!

What is Luxe's favorite dessert?

Karat cake!

Who looked super cute on the red carpet of the ultra-glitzy Golden Bowl Award

4

ART CLUB
LIVE IN COLOR!

They say that art imitates life, but Art Club B.B.s *create* life, and they leave their mark everywhere they go! For them, life is a canvas they use to express themselves. Whether it's with crayons, markers, brushes, or spray paint, these fabulous B.B.s make the world brilliant with a whole-lotta color!

You'll always win the race.

Do you think Scribbles takes things a little too far sometimes?

Yeah, he doesn't know where to draw the line!

AMPERED PET
urrfect Shapes dreams
f visiting Egypt to see
e pyramids because
e thinks they're the
erfect shape!

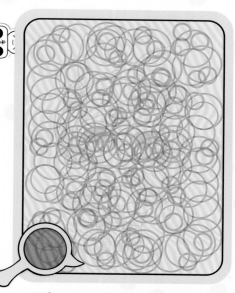

Who won the game of Red Light, Green Light?

CLUB MOTTO

SURPRISE!
Red is the first color that a baby can see!

SPLATTERS

SCRIBBLES

SHAPES

POP HEART

As long as you set your pace.

ATHLETIC CLUB
FIT TO BE GREAT!

Athletic Club B.B.s are all-stars! No one can stop them from going for the gold. These sporty superstars break records—and break hearts. On the court, on the field, and even on the ice, the adorable athletes are ready to play and, most importantly, have fun!

Everyone cheered when this B.B. shot a hole in one at the ultra-fancy Royal Greens course.

SPRINTS   **DRAG RACER**   **CADDY CUTIE**   **SK8ER GRRRL**

PAMPERED PET
Sur-fur Puppy loves surfing at Hanalei Bay in Hawaii, not just because the waves are awesome, but because this pretty beach town has the perfect, super chill vibe.

SURPRISE! Fenway Park in Boston is over 100 years old! B.B.s have always loved baseball.

Which animal is b at hitting baseball

A bat!

CHILL OUT CLUB
VACAY ALL THE WAY!

These supercool B.B.s travel the world looking for cool times. From shopping in Paris to snuggling by the fire with a cup of hot chocolate, they savor every jet-set moment! No matter the temperature, these superstars know how to have fun. So, take a deep breath, feel the mellow vibes of the Chill Out Club, and enjoy!

And know that you can achieve.

Where did the piano player go to vacay?

The Florida Keys!

COZY BABE **POSH** **BRRR B.B.** **SNOW ANGEL**

PAMPERED PET
Cozy Kitty loves visiting cat cafés around the world, especially the adorable Temari no Ouchi in Tokyo, Japan, because it's like being in a warm and comfy fairy-tale house!

CLUB MOTTO
Q.T. + 🛋 + 🕶

SURPRISE!
The record for the heaviest snowfall in one day is 100.8 inches in Italy in 2015. Talk about a snow day!

How did Snow Angel feel when she hit the ski slopes?

7

CLUB MOTTO

👗 + ▷▷

COSPLAY CLUB
DRESS TO EXPRESS!

Why be like the rest? That's what the Cosplay Club B.B.s say! Nothing's more fun than dressing up as their favorite characters or whoever they want to be. It's always time to stand out and shine. These super creative superstars are quick to celebrate their style and show what they love.

FANIME

BON BON

NEON Q.T.

MIDNIGHT

What did one hat say to the other hat?

Stay here, I'll go on ahead.

SURPRISE!
Kodomo anime is a Japanese art style made especially for kids. Don't miss a frame!

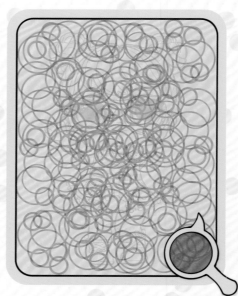

Who will be featured on the next cover of an anime magazine?

PAMPERED PE
Hop Hop is pretty in pink (and blue) and all ready to show off her fab style at comic-con!

To dream, to dance.

DANCE CLUB
DON'T WORRY, JUST DANCE!

When the music starts, these B.B.s are light on their feet and ready to sizzle on the dance floor! Dance Club is in the house, and there's no stopping the dazzling dancers from sliding, hip-hopping, breaking, and doing the shiggy on the dance floor or *any* floor!

Who kicked up their heels at the square dance contest?

DO-SI-DUDE

LINE DANCER

CENTER STAGE

SURPRISE!
Capoeira is a sporty Brazilian dance that combines dance and martial arts. It's a real dance battle!

Why didn't the skeleton go to the dance?

He had no body to dance with!

PAMPERED PET
After swinging and rocking out all night, Stage Owl relaxes with a warm bubble bath . . . till it's time to put on her dancing shoes again!

CLUB MOTTO

+

Now's your chance.

ELEKTRO CLUB
SPARKS OF FABULOUS!

Electrifying and cool, Elektro Club B.B.s are ready to hit the club scene in their high-stylin' outfits. Dressed in bright glittery colors and ultracool patterns, these high-energy B.B.s sparkle as they tear up the dance floor. It's showtime!

SURPRISE!
EDM stands for electronic dance music. Also known as club music, it was extremely popular in Europe before hitting it big in the United States.

E.D.M.B.B.

RAINBOW RAVER

PAMPERED PET
Born to scratch! The crowd goes wild whenever E.D.M. Scratch shows up to scratch vinyl at the clu

Why are Olympic athletes bad DJs?

Because they're always smashing records!

CLUB MOTTO
👊 + 2 +

Who showed up with kandi bracelets for all her friends at the music festival?

GLAM CLUB
GLAM LYFE!

It's showtime, B.B.s! These glittery, glam B.B.s sparkle in everything they do, from strutting in the latest style and making incredible ice sculptures to rocking the red carpet. They were born ready to take over the world with style.

The Glam B.B.s, they love to wow.

When is a piece of wood like Her Majesty?

When it's a ruler!

SURPRISE! Elton John, David Bowie, and the band Queen were part of the glam rock music movement that began in the 1960s.

CLUB MOTTO

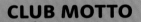

DOLLFACE   **HER MAJESTY**   **SHOWBABY**

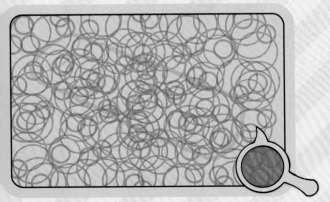

What did Showbaby forget when she rushed off to her big performance?

PAMPERED PET
Miss Skunk loves trying different perfumes, but her favorite is *Eau de Pew*.

GLEE CLUB
READY TO SING, READY TO BLING!

Born to sparkle and sing! No one can stop the Glee Club B.B.s from hitting the high notes. They're always on key, on stage or off. And when these divine superstars lift their voices up, they get everyone on their feet, inspiring and touching the hearts of all who love music.

Who had the crowd cheering for "more, more, more!" when she performed at Lollipoplooza?

SURPRISE!
More than one hundred muscles in your body work together when you speak or sing. Who knew chatting was a workout?

M.C. SWAG

ROCKER

DIVA

PAMPERED PET
80s Hog's favorite song is "Girls Just Want to Have Fun"!

Why did Diva climb a ladder during her song?

She wanted to reach the high notes!

GLITTERATI CLUB
GLITTER GLAM 4 LYFE!

It's *Lights! Glamour! Action!* with the Glitterati! These fierce B.B.s rock with their glitzy outfits and sparkling personalities. Whether they're walking the red carpet or dancing in the club, the Glitterati always bling it up. Every B.B. is welcome in the Glitterati, where everyone is family. All it takes is a sprinkle of twinkle and a little bit of shine.

Fresh and bold, they never whine.

SURPRISE! Ancient Egyptians used the bodies of beetles to create glitterlike makeup. Ewwwww!!

What is Bling Queen's favorite accessory?

PAMPERED PET
Kitty Kitty loves all kinds of tunes, but her favorite is pop mew-sic.

What is Cosmic Queen's favorite weather?

Reign!

BLING QUEEN

KITTY QUEEN

KAWAII QUEEN

COSMIC QUEEN

Glitterati rise and shine.

GLITTER BOMB!

To help you spark your inner glow.

HIP HOP CLUB
CRAZY COOL SUPERSTARS!

You gotta work it! From old school to new school, hip hop is a universal language that's all about expressing yourself and being true to you. Hip Hop Club B.B.s welcome everyone from the city, country, and everywhere in between. It's not about where you're from, it's about where you are!

What did Shorty get from one of her biggest fans?

D.J.

SHORTY

HONEY BUN

BEATS

What kind of music do bunnies like?

Hip hop, of course!

SURPRISE!
The hip-hop scene is more than just rapping. It's also about deejaying, graffiti painting, and dancing, too!

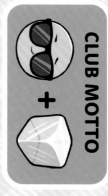

CLUB MOTTO

What did the mama broom say to the baby broom?

NAP CLUB

SHHHHH . . .

Dim the lights, it's naptime. And these pets know just what they need for a perfect snooze: a comfy bed, warm milk, soothing music, and . . . *yawn* . . . time to catch some *zzz*'s.

It's time to go to sweep.

CLUB MOTTO

PAMPERED PET
Kittydoll loves to curl up with a good book.

SURPRISE!
Cats spend more than 60 percent of their lives sleeping.

LE SKUNK BÉBÉ

KITTYDOLL

What's the Nap Club's favorite time other than naptime?

SLEEPING BARKY

SLEEPY BUNS

OPPOSITES CLUB
AWESOME FROM START TO FINISH!

Who's spicy and sweet while burnin' hot and super chill? Opposites Club is all about daring to be yourself, even if that makes you different. These snazzy and sassy B.B.s are not shy about showing who they are and steppin' out to lead the pack from the front or from the back!

Bring on the heat, Fyre and Ice.

What goes up, but never comes down?

My age.

DAWN

DUSK

SUGAR

SPICE

What message did the Opposites Club put in everyone's swag bag?

PAMPERED PET
Fancy Haute Dog loves to go window-shopping in the big city and look at all the bling!

CLUB MOTTO

SURPRISE!
Hot fact! Flammable and inflammable look like opposites, but they both mean the same thing: easily set on fire.

Stars like Fierce are really nice.

POP CLUB
BFFS 4 LYFE!

Pop Club B.B.s are fresh and fabulous! The spotlight shines bright on these supercool divas. When they're not onstage singing their hearts out, these friends keep on groovin' and movin' wherever they are.

Who wowed everyone at her photo shoot?

DARING DIVA

80S B.B.

FIERCE

I keep hearing music coming from the printer.

I think the paper's jamming!

SURPRISE!
The word "pop" in "pop music" is short for popular. It's music that makes *a lot* of people happy!

CLUB MOTTO

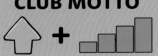

CLUB MOTTO
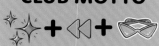

Miss Jive keeps things fresh and new.

RETRO CLUB
OLD-SCHOOL COOL!

Nostalgia overload! The irresistible Retro Club B.B.s go back in time and make the past cool and fresh. Vintage vibes and chic styles give these funky superstars a look that's off the hook.

Who received a standing ovation when she read her poems at RetroFest?

PAMPERED PET
Turn up the music! Jitter Critter's favorite dance is the bunny hop!

What do cars do at the disco?

SURPRISE!
The Lindy Hop, jive, jitterbug, and boogie-woogie are names of swing dances that were popular a hundred years ago.

They brake dance!

MISS JIVE

SOUL BABE

CHERRY

BEATNIK BABE

Cheeky Babe is so true blue.

ROCK CLUB
EAT. SLEEP. ROCK!

From classic rock to funk and punk rock, the amazing Rock Club is legendary! Whether they're on tour or just jamming in their living rooms, these ultracool B.B.s make riffing on guitar strings and performing look easy. So, pull on those boots and rock on!

CLUB MOTTO

 +2+ 🐝 + 😺

Why did Grunge Grrrl sit on the rocking chair with roller skates on?

She wanted to rock and roll!

PAMPERED PET
Funky Kat's favorite singer is Elton John.

SURPRISE!
In Argentina, a man planted a forest in the shape of a guitar. He used blue trees for the strings!

Who was chosen to play for the royal family when they visited?

GRUNGE GRRRL   **PUNK BOI**   **FUNKY Q.T.**   **CHEEKY BABE**

SLEEPOVER CLUB
CUDDLY AND CUTE!

Any day is a good day for a sleepover. This *zzzzz*-ful club knows that there's nothing more fun than snuggling in your jammies, chilling with your besties, and falling asleep all comfy and cozy. These B.B.s party till it's bedtime and rock on in their dreams!

Sleepy B.B.s make no sound.

If you had a pet cow, where would it sleep?

On the COWch, of course!

SLEEPY BONES   **BABYDOLL**   **SLEEPING B.B.**   **SNUGGLE BABE**

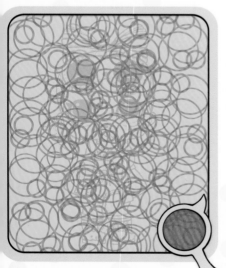

Who sang a special lullaby at the Sleepover Club's last sleepover?

PAMPERED PET
Sleepy Buns looks forward to sleepovers; that's when she gets extra-special treats!

CLUB MOTTO

SURPRISE!
In ancient times, people made pillows out of wood or stone. That's one way to rock yourself to sleep!

SURPRISE!

Rah! The largest cheerleader routine ever had 2,102 people from ages five to sixty-eight cheering!

SPIRIT CLUB
C-H-A-M-P-S!

Two, four, six, eight! Who do we celebrate? Majorette, Teacher's Pet, Cheer Captain! Start clappin'!
Always cheerful and eager to learn, these dynamic go-getters energize everyone around them, on the field and off. Go, team, go!

TEAM

GO TEAM

GO TEAM

01

MAJORETTE

CHEER CAPTAIN

LIL CHEER CAPTAIN

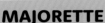

CLUB MOTTO

 + RAD

PAMPERED PET

Teacher's Hoot's favorite book is *Owl Moon*, a story about a girl and her dad who go looking for owls one winter night.

How did the marching band fix the broken tuba?

With a tuba glue!

Who led her band to victory in the marching band competition?

¡ooꓭ

SPOOKY CLUB
CREEPY COOL RULES!

Every day is Halloween for these sensational Spooky Club superstars! Candy, pranks, and partying with friends? It doesn't get any better than this. These super mysterious and supercute B.B.s know just how to scare up some good times!

Who won the first prize with her phenomenal entry at the pumpkin-carving contest?

CLUB MOTTO
PAMPERED PET

Cuervo Bonito loves snuggling next to Bebé Bonita and listening to spine-tingling stories. The spookier the tale, the better!

SURPRISE!
Centuries ago, the Irish carved turnips on All Hallows' Eve instead of pumpkins! B.B.s love some little, outrageous jack-o'-lanterns!

What is Lil Thrilla's favorite dessert?

I scream!

| COUNTESS | THRILLA | WITCHAY BABAY | BEBÉ BONITA |

CLUB MOTTO

Who won first place at the science fair?

S.T.E.M. CLUB
ALWAYS BE CURIOUS!

The S.T.E.M. Club is ready to turn on the brainpower! These supersmart B.B.s know that every day brings an opportunity to learn something new. There's always something waiting to be discovered. They're ready to ask questions, discover, and create in order to come up with something brand sparkling new.

V.R.Q.T.

GLAMSTRONAUT

CAN DO BABY

P.H.D.B.B.

SURPRISE!
The Earth is called the "Blue Planet" because it looks like a pale blue dot from space. That's because oceans make up about 75 percent of the Earth's surface.

What did the science book say to the math book?

Wow, do you have problems!

PAMPERED PET
When the full moon is out, Racoon-stronaut's heart is full as well. Wolf moon, snow moon, pink moon, and strawberry moon—she loves them all!

CLUB MOTTO

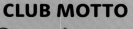

Who brought the most number of books to the read-a-thon?

STORYBOOK CLUB
FABULOUSLY EPIC!

Storybook Club B.B.s love a good tale and have many exciting stories to share! Curling up on the couch with a classic story are these imaginative B.B.s' idea of a magical way to spend their days—and nights! The stories they read take them to many different places and help them connect with each other. They're best book buddies 4 lyfe!

SURPRISE!
The phrase "once upon a time" has been the opening line for stories dating as far back as the thirteenth century. That means there are a lot of happily ever afters!

PAMPERED PET
Cottontail Q.T.'s favorite book is *The Runaway Bunny*. She just loves happy endings!

Which building in the city has the most stories?

The library.

KANSAS Q.T.   **GOODIE**   **CURIOUS Q.T.**   **TINZ**

Rip Tide always rules the swim meet.

CLUB MOTTO

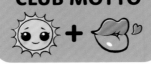

SWIM CLUB
COOL IN THE POOL!

Whether it's a pool or the sea, in the water is where Swim Club B.B.s want to be! These amazing aqua B.B.s have a fin-tastic time and are always ready to make a splash.

What did Waves bring home from the swim competition?

RIP TIDE

VACAY BABAY

WAVES

SURPRISE!
Free divers don't use scuba gear when they swim underwater. They can hold their breath for 10 minutes!

What did Cinderella wear when she went swimming?

Glass flippers!

PAMPERED PET
Hammy Tide loves nothing more than lying on her favorite beach towel and listening to the sound of the waves. So relaxing!

THEATER CLUB
SHINE BRIGHT!

All the world's a stage for these superstars! The Theater Club is always *on*, even when they're not in front of an audience. They've got their lines down, and they won't be upstaged. These B.B.s stay in the spotlight until it's time to take a bow and leave their audience wanting more.

Raising B.B.s to new heights.

CLUB MOTTO

MERBABY   **COCONUT Q.T.**   **ANGEL**   **UNICORN**

Who got the lead role in the Theater Club's latest play?

PAMPERED PET
Su-prr Kitty is a great understudy. When one of the actors can't perform, she's always ready to step in and save the show.

Did you hear about the time Lil Pharaoh Babe fell through the floor during a show?

Yeah. She was going through a stage.

SURPRISE!
The smallest theater in the world is in Austria. The stage is only four feet wide by four feet deep, and there are only eight seats in the audience.

27

TINY TOYS

STROBE B.B. BOT

JUKE BOT

LASER

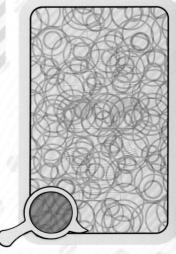

Who was in charge of turning on the lights at the holiday lights festival?

BOOG-E 300 CLUB

BRIGHT LIGHTS, GLITZY BOTS!

The Boog-E 300 Club lights up the night—and day—with their shimmer and shine. These bots turn on the wow factor everywhere they go. Full of energy, they are all juiced up and ready to bounce!

QT FI CLUB

IT'S TIME TO BE FAB!

Glitzy and glamorous, the QT FI Club puts on the ritz and motivates B.B.s to get up and work it! Always ready to make exciting connections, these fabulous B.B.s have gigabytes of love to share.

X-TENSIONS　　**BB K155**　　**POWDER UP**

SURPRISE! Alpha Dog is a four-legged robot created by scientists to carry equipment in dangerous places. That's some ruff work!

Dressed up and down in shorts or gowns.

What surprise did SPF 0 get from her BFF?

SPF 0

SURPRISE!

The sun is about 93 million miles away from Earth. At that distance, it takes a little over eight minutes for sunlight to reach our planet.

SOLAR POWER CLUB
SHIMMER ON, SUNSHINE!

Put on your shades, Solar Power Club is in the house! B.B.s like SPF 0 are powered by the sun and always shine bright.

SPACE SQUAD CLUB
COSMIC MEGASTARS!

The Space Squad Club is ready for action! These stellar B.B.s shine wherever they go and in everything they do. They love meeting B.B.s and making friends. After all, it's friends who make the world go 'round.

What did the robot do when it was time for lunch?

He had a byte.

ORBIT　　**MOON WALKER**　　**ROCKET**

TAKE A BOW!

From big cities to tiny towns.

GO TEAM

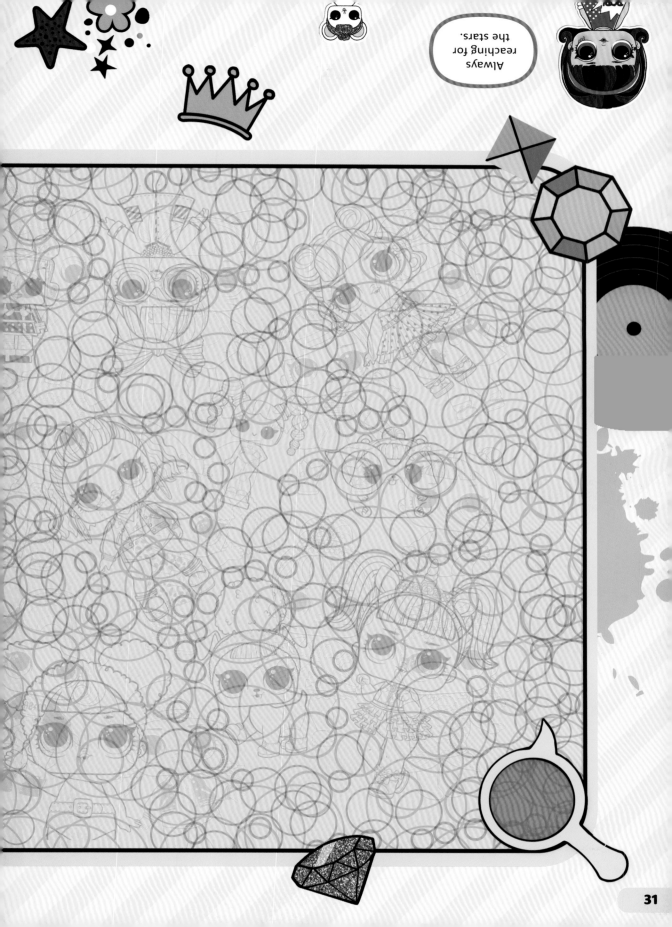

You've reached the end, now start again!

Stylin' B.B.s, that's who we are.

HIDE OR SQUEAK
Sugar Squeak is a bit of a bookworm. She's hiding on every page of this book. Did you find her? Better go back and look!

MAKE YOUR OWN SLEEPOVER CLUB MINI BOOK!

CREATE A LIBRARY FOR YOUR L.O.L. SURPRISE! DOLLS

What you'll need: a stapler.
(That's it! We provide the rest.)
How to make your mini book:

1. Carefully remove the column of mini book pages on the right. Lay the pages down on a table in the order they are numbered in the guide.

   a. Place page 1 down first, with the text facing up, like the guide.

   b. Place page 2 on top of page 1.

   c. Place page 3 on top of page 2, and continue with the other pages.

   d. When you're done, the cover should be at the top of the pile of pages.

2. Slide the stack of papers into your stapler. Position the line between the front and back covers under the staple. Press down on the stapler so the staple goes in on that line.

3. With your thumb on the front cover and forefinger on the back cover, fold the stack of pages along that line with the staple in it.

Congratulations, B.B.s! You've just made your dolls their very own lullaby storybook.

Time to snuggle and get cozy.	**1**	Super B.B. and Luxe too,
Like Queen Bee, Tinsel, Stardust Queen?	**2**	Glitter Queen and Honey Bun,
Resting B.B.s say good night.	**3**	Twinkle, twinkle superstars,

4 SHINE BRIGHT

Time to snuggle and get cozy.

Super B.B. and Luxe too,

Like Queen Bee, Tinsel, Stardust Queen?

Glitter Queen and Honey Bun,

Resting B.B.s say good night.

Twinkle, twinkle superstars,

SHINE BRIGHT

37

Sparkle, sparkle just for you.

Prezzie and sweet Sleeping B.B.,

1

Sparkle, sparkle just for you.

Prezzie and sweet Sleeping B.B.,

Shine like diamonds in the sun.

Won't you close your eyes and dream,

2

Shine like diamonds in the sun.

Won't you close your eyes and dream,

Look how glittery you are!

Twinkle, twinkle shine so bright,

3

Look how glittery you are!

Twinkle, twinkle shine so bright,

4

© MGA

MAKE YOUR OWN STORYBOOK CLUB MINI BOOK!

CREATE A LIBRARY FOR YOUR L.O.L. SURPRISE! DOLLS

What you'll need: a stapler.
(That's it! We provide the rest.)
How to make your mini book:

1. Carefully remove the column
   of mini book pages on the
   right. Lay the pages down on
   a table in the order they are
   numbered in the guide.

   a. Place page 1 down first,
      with the text facing up,
      like the guide.

   b. Place page 2 on top
      of page 1.

   c. Place page 3 on top of
      page 2, and continue with
      the other pages.

   d. When you're done, the
      cover should be at the top
      of the pile of pages.

2. Slide the stack of papers into
   your stapler. Position the line
   between the front and back
   covers under the staple. Press
   down on the stapler so the
   staple goes in on that line.

3. With your thumb on the front
   cover and forefinger on the
   back cover, fold the stack of
   pages along that line with the
   staple in it.

Congratulations, B.B.s! You've
just made your dolls their very
own storybook.

"It's such a lovely day," Kansas Q.T. said. "There's no reason to rush."

1

"I can get there faster than you," Sprints said, as she started running to the right.

Just as they knocked on Cherry's door, Sprints and Roller Sk8er showed up!

2

"Where are you going?" Sprints asked.

The moral: Chill and steady is a perfect pace.

3

One day, Kansas Q.T. and Kansas K9 set off to bring a basket of treats to Cherry.

4

LITTLE RED IN THE HOOD

1 "I'll be there way before you!" said Roller Sk8er, skating to the left.

But Kansas Q.T. knew her path was a shortcut and continued walking straight ahead.

2 "To Cherry's house," said Kansas Q.T. "There's no place like her home."

Kansas K9 barked in agreement, and they reached the house before long.

3 As they walked through the park, they met Sprints and Roller Sk8er.

"Surprise!" everyone yelled when Cherry opened the door.

4

CLUB MOTTOS

24K GOLD
Hearts of Gold

ART
Paint the Town

ATHLETIC
Game, Set, Glam!

CHILL OUT
Cutie, Cozy, Cool

COSPLAY
Fashion Forward

DANCE
Dance Til Dawn

ELEKTRO
Ready to Party

GLAM
Selfie Ready

GLEE
Sing Out, B.B.s!

GLITTERATI
Sugar, Spice, and
Everything Sparkle

HIP-HOP
Cool as Ice

NAP
Hush Lil' B.B.s

OPPOSITES
Playtime Rain
or Shine

POP
Top of the Charts

RETRO
Flashback Fierce

ROCK
Born to Be Bad

SLEEPOVER
At Ease

SPIRIT
Rah Rah Radical!

SPOOKY
Spooky Ookie

S.T.E.M.
Smart Cookies

STORYBOOK
Fairytale Fierce

SWIM
Sun Kissed

THEATER
Showtime!

INSIGHT KIDS

An Imprint of Insight Editions
PO Box 3088
San Rafael, CA 94912
www.insighteditions.com

Find us on Facebook: www.facebook.com/InsightEditions
Follow us on Twitter: @insighteditions

Library of Congress Cataloging-in-Publication Data available.

ISBN: 978-1-64722-110-2

Publisher: Raoul Goff
President: Kate Jerome
Associate Publisher: Vanessa Lopez
Creative Director: Chrissy Kwasnik
VP of Manufacturing: Alix Nicholaeff
Junior Designer: Brooke McCullum
Senior Editor: Paul Ruditis
Editorial Assistant: Samantha Johnson
Managing Editor: Lauren LePera
Production Editor: Jennifer Bentham
Senior Production Manager: Greg Steffen

Insight Kids would like to thank Elizabeth Ovieda for her editorial assistance on this project.

 ROOTS of PEACE   REPLANTED PAPER

Insight Editions, in association with Roots of Peace, will plant two trees for each tree used in the
manufacturing of this book. Roots of Peace is an internationally renowned humanitarian organization
dedicated to eradicating land mines worldwide and converting war-torn lands into productive farms and
wildlife habitats. Roots of Peace will plant two million fruit and nut trees in Afghanistan and provide farmers
there with the skills and support necessary for sustainable land use.

Manufactured in China by Insight Editions

10 9 8 7 6 5 4 3 2 1